Foreword

Debra Ende's book is remarkable. It is both insightful and useful, by far the most practical resource I have ever used with children when introducing and discussing the concept of Asperger's syndrome.

It is humorous and invites children to contribute to the discussion about Asperger's syndrome. It clearly sets out how people can be the same yet different.

Many children with Asperger's syndrome find it difficult and lack the words to express their experience. This book is extraordinarily helpful in introducing the concept of Asperger's syndrome and provides children with a vocabulary to describe their unique way of viewing the world, a vocabulary which they can make their own.

I have had the opportunity of using this resource and have found that children treasure the concepts outlined in this book, especially the extended metaphor of different operating systems.

I read this book with a child who was unaware that he had Asperger's syndrome. Whilst we were reading the book, he promptly informed me that he had a 'half-half' system. He was halfway between the Standard Operating System and the Asperger's Operating System. The child had adopted the concepts in the book, internalised them and used them in his own unique way.

The book also provides practical tips and solutions, especially on how to deal with system 'crashes'. This allows children to understand why they are having 'crashes' and gives them the tools needed to reboot their systems and deal with the consequences.

This story provides a voice and understanding of what it can be like to have an Asperger's Operating System. This book will appeal to individual students who may read it alone, with a counsellor or with parents or carers at home. It can also be used in the classroom.

Margriet Horvath
School Counsellor/ Educational Psychologist

For David and his mother

Acknowledgements

Firstly, I would like to acknowledge the invaluable contribution of my former colleague, Dannielle Wilson, who was involved in working with me on the first version of this book.

I am also very appreciative of the warm interest and guidance of my editor, Annemarie Rolls, who made the experience of bringing my book to publication such a rewarding one.

I would also like to thank, Carol Gray, for permission to use the Asperger's Operating System analogy from the article by Ellen Tanis published in *The Morning News*, Fall 1996, p.15.

Finally, I would like to pay tribute to the many children and their families whom I have met and been involved with over the years. I have so often been delighted to be in their company and I continue to learn from them.

Making Sense of Asperger's

A story for children

Written by **Debra Ende**
Illustrated by **Bettina Guthridge**

All of us are the same.

WHY?

Because we are all people.

But ... we are also each different.

No two people are ever exactly the same.

WHY?

Because each of us is an individual.

There are many different things which make us ourselves.

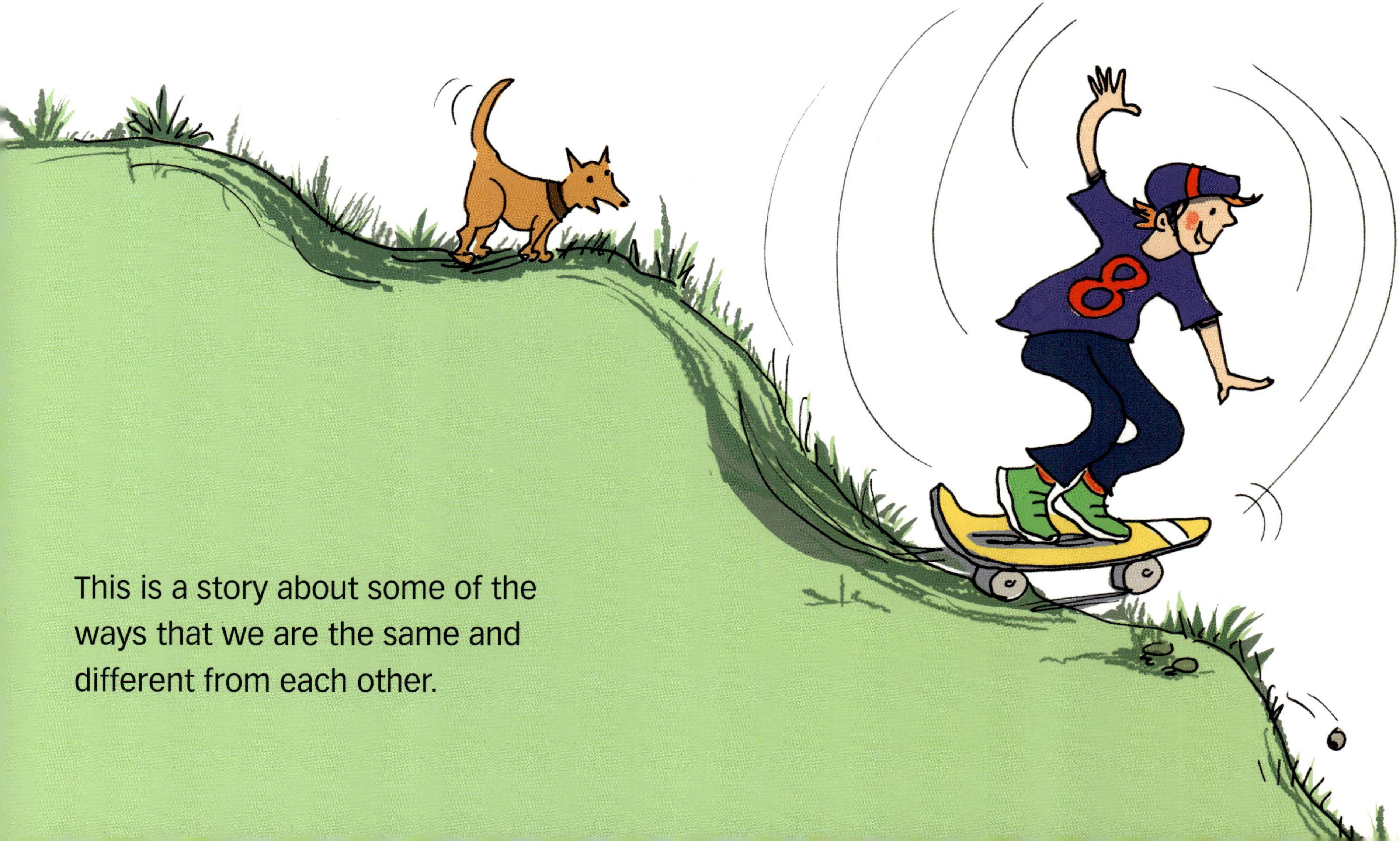

This is a story about some of the ways that we are the same and different from each other.

Some of the ways that we are different we can see from the outside of a person.

These are things like:

* how tall we are – big or small
* whether we are a boy or a girl
* what colour our skin is.

There are also differences which we cannot see from the outside of a person.

These are things like:

* who our favourite teacher is
* whether or not we enjoy playing chess
* how we feel during thunderstorms
* who our worst enemy is.

Another really important way that people are different is the way in which we make sense of everything. That is, all the things we see and hear, feel and think.

We could think of this as being a bit like how an **OPERATING SYSTEM** works inside a computer.

The operating system helps the computer to make sense of all the information that is put into it.

Then the operating system produces what we see on the screen.

And, there are different operating systems for different kinds of computers.

For example, with PCs and Apple® computers:

- The operating system for a PC is called Windows®.

- The operating system for an Apple® is called Mac OS®.

Both operating systems make the computers work, but each system works in a different way.

It is the same for people.
That is, people can also have different kinds of operating systems.

This means that we make sense of what we see, hear, feel and think in different ways, partly depending on what kind of human operating system we have.

We could think of the operating system which most people have as a **STANDARD OPERATING SYSTEM**.

What is a Standard Operating System like?

Well, a person who has this kind of operating system usually:

- thinks about things in words
- may like surprises
- knows what to do and what the rules are when there are groups of people together, like in the playground or at a birthday party

* may quite like changes and doesn't mind too much if things change quickly
* doesn't mind loud noises or strong smells
* finds many different topics interesting
* likes to play with others most of the time
* often enjoys lots of people being together at the same time.

There is also another kind of operating system that people can have.

A person with this operating system usually:

- makes sense of things by thinking in pictures
- mostly likes things to be in their right place and right order
- feels happy when things stay the same

- notices patterns in things very quickly and easily, like the times tables
- gets really interested in just one topic at a time, and likes to think and talk about that topic a lot
- wants everyone to follow the rules exactly

* doesn’t like things to change quickly or without warning
* has a very good memory and remembers things in very clear detail

* really likes to get everything right and feels worried when they don’t know something
* may prefer to play by themselves or with only one or two other people

* may need lots of time alone to think about things and settle down
* gets upset with too much noise.

This type of operating system has a special name.
It is called an **ASPERGER’S OPERATING SYSTEM.**

Which operating system do you think you might have?

What about other people you know?

As we can see, even though these two **operating systems** are mostly different, each one has lots of really great things.

Also, some things may be easier for people with a Standard Operating System, and other things may be easier for people with an Asperger's Operating System.

Another way to think about it is that whichever operating system we have, we all like to have fun – but we might have different ideas about what fun is for us!

Draw something that's fun for **you** …

FUN FOR ME

When you have an Asperger's Operating System things can get tricky

Even though there are some really good things about having an Asperger's Operating System sometimes things can also get really tricky.

WHY?

Most places we go to are set up for people who have a Standard Operating System and many people don't know that there can be other operating systems as well.

Also, because some parts of the Asperger's Operating System and the Standard Operating System aren't in the same format, sometimes they just don't get on together easily.

When do things get tricky?

Things may get tricky when:

* something is not in its right place
* things change too quickly or without enough warning
* there are too many people all together
* you feel really worried, stressed or tired – like after school
* someone else doesn't follow the rules exactly
* it gets too noisy or there is too much talking
* you're not sure what someone wants you to do and you're worried you might not get it right.

Crashes

If you have an Asperger's Operating System and things get tricky or go wrong, sometimes you can get very upset very, very quickly.

Then, sometimes, you can even have a

CRASH! … just like a computer does!

When there is a crash, everything stops working for a little while.

It's hard to think or use your words in a helpful way to try and work things out.

Sometimes you can even be really silly, shout at others, use rude words or hurt other people, which can get you into big trouble.

People sometimes call these crashes a meltdown.

After the crash is over …
you may often feel very sad or upset.

This is because you have not really wanted to be naughty or rude, or to hurt other people.

But somehow once it has started, it can be very difficult to stop a crash.

Once we know that someone has an Asperger's Operating System there are things we can do to help so that the crashes don't happen so often and everyone can get on better.

Trying to stop crashes before they happen

When you know you have an Asperger's Operating System, you can learn the warning signs which you can often feel inside you just before a crash is about to happen.

These warning signs can be things like:

* your head begins to hurt
* your shoulders begin to feel tight
* your throat starts feeling dry
* your armpits get sweaty
* your hands curl up into fists
* your knees begin to wobble.

The important thing is to learn to notice these warning signs. Once you begin to do this, when they happen you can try to:

* slowly count to five
* take some deep breaths
* find something else to do
* go and sit in a quiet place until you feel better.

This may help you to stop the crash from happening at all.

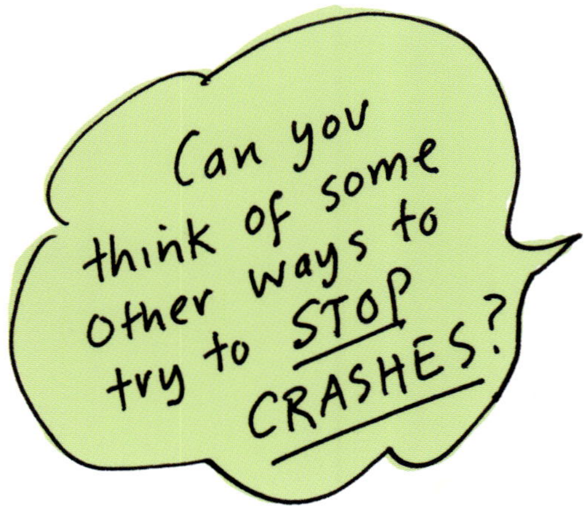

When a crash has already happened

If you haven't been able to recognise the warning signs and stop the crash, that's okay.

It can still be helpful to do something that makes you feel calm and safe again, like:

- taking some deep breaths
- sitting in a quiet place.

What else could you do to feel better after a crash?

When you feel OK again you can:

- say sorry (if you need to)
- accept any consequences (if you need to)

- move on and leave the **'crash** in the **trash'**.

But remember ...

When boys and girls with an Asperger's Operating System have a crash this is not the same as sometimes being a bit naughty.

People of all ages, with all kinds of operating systems, can be naughty for lots of reasons.

When this happens then there may have to be a consequence. This might be time-out, or losing some time on the computer.

Then, when the consequence is over, you can do fun things again.

Now we have come to the end of this story about all of us, about some of the things which makes each one of us the same but also different from each other.

When we are able to know and understand the operating system we each have inside us, then it is so much easier for us all to get on and be friends.